Hello, Tree!

by Joanne Ryder

illustrated by Michael Hays

Dutton   Lodestar Books   New York

for Franche Yep, with love,
and in memory of Thomas Gim Yep,
who loved his garden and made it a special place
J.R.

to the village of Oak Park
M.H.

Michael Hays ©91

One day
you will find
a tree
standing tall
in the sun
hiding secrets
in its branches
and feel
that this tree
is special
to you.

Come close
and see the way
your tree grows—
reaching up
toward clouds and sky
or spilling over
like a leafy waterfall.

Your tree
makes
its own
shadow
for you
to sit
within.
Here
it is cool
and good
to rest.

Above you,
patches of sky
peek through
the leaves
dancing in the wind.
Around you,
patches of sunlight
dance on the ground.

Listen
to the wind
blowing,
shhhhhhhhing
through
the treetop.
As branches sway
and leaves touch,
you can hear
your tree's voice
and listen to
the songs it sings.

If you find
a climbing tree,
reach up
and make
your way
with care
among the
crooked limbs
until you find
a snug one
all your own.
Lean back,
hold on,
and feel
your tree
hugging you
gently, firmly
in its strong
branches.

You sit
up high,
dangling
your legs,
free of the
brown ground
far below.

Inside your tree,
you are tall
looking out
at the world,
stretching
this way
and that,
seeing farther
than you could
ever see alone.

Around you,
branches curl
and twigs droop
with leaves.
Some trees have
leaves like mittens
or spear points
or tiny, dainty fans.
Some trees have
leaves like needles.
Touch a soft leaf
or long needle
hanging down.
Trace its shape
with your finger
and hold it
in your hand.

A tree tells you
its name
by its shape
and the shape
of its leaves.
Maple or oak
willow or pine
ginkgo or sassafras.

Your tree is alive
and full
of living things.
Some live here.
Some visit
just like you.
Your tree
is a pathway
from one place
to another.

And it is
a home.
Look and see
who comes
to visit
and who
peeks out
watching you
visit it.

As you climb down,
feel the
smoothness,
the roughness
of your tree's
hard skin.
Step gently
on the twisting roots
that reach
underground
deeper and deeper
holding your tree
keeping it safe.

Your tree may be
young or very old,
but here it has made
its home in the world.
On a hill, in a yard
by a lake, in a field,
each tree lives
and grows in its
own special place.

Your tree shares
its home with you
so you can play
or rest here,
watching the world
all around.

It's good
to remember
this place
and your tree.

So even when
the leaves
have changed color
or fallen to the ground—
you will know
your tree
from any other.
You will feel it
waiting
like a friend
for you
to come again.
And you'll run
calling softly,
Hello, tree!

You will hear
its branches
whispering
its own song.
You will sit
inside its shade
and look out
just as before
and see how much
the world
has changed too.

And even when
you've grown
older and taller,
you'll look up
again and see
your tree
is taller still.

It's good
to know a tree
and good to find
that old friends
grow along
together
year
    after year
        after year.

Library of Congress Cataloging-in-Publication Data

Ryder, Joanne.
     Hello, Tree!/by Joanne Ryder; illustrated by Michael Hays.—
1st ed.
         p.   cm.
     Summary: Describes, in simple text and illustrations,
some of the unique characteristics of trees.
     ISBN 0-525-67310-5
     1. Trees—Juvenile literature.   [1. Trees.]
I. Hays, Michael, 1956– ill.   II. Title.
QK475.8.R93   1991
582.16—dc20
89-13343   CIP   AC

Published in the United States by Lodestar Books,
an affiliate of Dutton Children's Books,
a division of Penguin Books USA Inc.

Published simultaneously in Canada by
McClelland & Stewart, Toronto

Editor: Virginia Buckley
Designer: Marilyn Granald, LMD

Printed in Hong Kong

First Edition   10 9 8 7 6 5 4 3 2